Adapted by David Lewman

Based on the episode "Truck or Treat" by Morgan von Ancken

Illustrated by Jason Fruchter

A GOLDEN BOOK • NEW YORK

randomhousekids.com

ISBN 978-1-5247-1669-1

Printed in the United States of America

10 9 8 7 6 5 4 3 2 1

It was Halloween night in Axle City, and the Monster Machines were wearing their costumes.

"Truck or treat!" shouted Sir Blaze and Superhero AJ when Lion Gabby answered her door.

"Happy Halloween!" roared Gabby, and she dropped candy into their buckets.

Blaze and AJ raced down the street to get more candy.

"Look! All our friends are truck-or-treating, too," said AJ. Starla was dressed as a witch. Zeg was a king. Stripes wore a pirate costume, and Darington was an octopus.

"Nice costumes, guys!" said Blaze. Everyone looked great.

Darington noticed something nearby. "Oh, that guy's got a costume just like mine," he said.

"That's not someone in a costume," replied Blaze. "That's your shadow!" He and AJ explained that when your body blocks a light source, it makes a shadow.

The Monster Machines made shadows in Blaze's bright light. When AJ held up his superhero cape, his shadow looked like a big, spooky bat!

Meanwhile, Crusher and Pickle were driving along a nearby street.

"Halloween is the best," said Pickle. "You get to wear a costume, stay out late, and get candy. Just look at all the candy Blaze and his friends have!"

"Oooh, I want their candy!" Crusher whispered greedily. "And I know just how to get it. I'm going truck-or-*cheating*! Heh-heh-heh . . ."

Crusher built a Halloween Candy Stealer.

The machine started sucking up the other trucks' Halloween candy buckets. But before long, it began to bulge and smoke. It was going to break!

"Um, Candy Stealer," Crusher said, worried, "you can stop now!"

But the Candy Stealer kept sucking up buckets until— *KABOOM!* It blew up, shooting the buckets of candy into the sky.

Blaze and his pals heard the loud explosion. "Look!" cried Starla. "Our candy's flyin' away!" Then they spotted Crusher speeding after the flying buckets!

"That's *our* candy!" said Darington.
"We worked really hard truck-or-treating to get it," said Stripes.

"We've got to hurry and get our candy back before Crusher gets it," said Blaze. "AJ, give me some speed!"

Blaze and his friends drove after the candy. Using his Visor View, AJ spotted the buckets on some hay bales next to a barn outside Axle City.

"We've got to get to that barn before Crusher does!" Blaze said. *ZOOM!* They roared toward the barn.

The fog that night was so thick that Stripes, Zeg, Starla, and Darington got separated from Blaze. They ended up driving right into a big mud pit.

"Oh, no!" cried Stripes. "This mud is really, really sticky!"

"How are we going to get our candy now?" asked Starla.

"Blaze!" they called. "HELP! We're stuck in the mud!"

"Don't worry!" Blaze shouted. "We'll get you out of there."

"How are we going to save them, with all this fog?" asked AJ.

Blaze had an idea. "Let's use shadows to find our friends," he said. "The light from the moon is shining down. And anything that blocks light makes a shadow."

Blaze spotted the shadow of Starla's pointy witch hat and used his tow hook to pull her out of the mud.

"You fellers saved me!" she said.

"Guys!" Stripes called. "I'm over here!"

AJ and Blaze looked for the shadow of the pirate sword Stripes was carrying. When they saw it, Blaze shot his tow hook into the fog and pulled Stripes out of the mud.

"All right!" AJ yelled. "We got him!"

"Yoo-hoo!" Zeg called. "Zeg over here!"
AJ saw the shadow of Zeg's crown and told Blaze to shoot his hook toward it. With a mighty tug, he pulled Zeg out of the mud.

"Yippee!" Zeg cheered. "You save Zeg!"

That left only Darington. AJ pointed at a shadow, and Blaze shot his hook into the fog. Blaze pulled so hard that Darington sailed through the air, did a flip, and landed right next to the other Monster Machines!

"Thanks for rescuing us," Darington said gratefully.

"You're welcome, guys," Blaze answered. "Now we've got to get our candy back!"

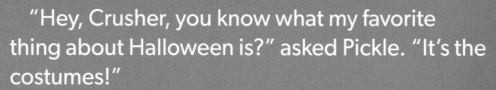

"Hey, Crusher, you know what my favorite thing about Halloween is?" asked Pickle. "It's the costumes!"

"Not me," said Crusher. "I just want the candy!"

Suddenly, a big shadow appeared on a rock near Crusher. He thought it was a scary monster! But it was just Pickle in his new costume—he was a butterfly! Then Crusher and Pickle heard Blaze's horn.

"Oh, no! They're trying to get their candy back!" cried Crusher. "If only there were some way to stop them . . ." He stomped his tire, and some rocks fell from a crack in the canyon wall. That gave him an idea.

Crusher hit the crack in the canyon wall with his tire. *RUMBLE! BOOM!* Rocks fell into a huge pile, blocking the path around the mountain!

Zeg tried to push the rocks out of the way, but they wouldn't budge. Then AJ spotted a big tree limb that had fallen.

"I think there's something behind that branch," said Blaze. He pushed the branch aside—and they saw a tunnel!
"Come on, everybody," said Blaze. "This way!"

The tunnel cut through the mountain, but it was full of tickling spiders! Starla and Zeg were laughing so hard, they couldn't drive.

"Hubcaps! Let's get out of here!" Blaze shouted. He and Stripes used their tow hooks to haul Starla and Zeg away from the spiders.

"Blaze, look!" said AJ. "Those spiders are making a giant web. We'll be trapped!"

VROOM! Blaze and his friends sped up and jumped through the web before it was finished. Soon they were out of the tunnel.

"Great job, everyone!" said Blaze. "This way to our candy!"

Meanwhile, Pickle had changed into another costume. Now he was dressed as a shoe! He raced after Crusher, who was heading toward the barn and the buckets of candy.

"It's Blaze again!" said Pickle. The Monster Machine and his friends were close!

"I've got to think up some way to *really* stop those guys this time," Crusher said. He looked around and spotted a pile of pumpkins. "I've got it!"

Crusher opened his hatch. Some parts flew out and snapped together.

FWOOM!

"Blaze and his buddies will never get past my Robo Pumpkin Launcher!" Crusher chuckled.

The machine hurled a metal Robo Pumpkin into the sky . . . right at Blaze and his friends!

WHAM! SMASH! As the Robo Pumpkins crashed to the ground, Blaze and the other Monster Machines took cover behind piles of hay.

"We need to engineer some way to get past those Robo Pumpkins," said Blaze. Starla suggested they use something to chop the pumpkins out of the sky.

"Hey, I know a machine that can do that," said AJ. "A reciprocating saw!" The others looked puzzled.

"It's a mechanical saw with a powerful moving blade."

"Yeah!" Blaze agreed. "Let's build a reciprocating saw!" First they made the sharp saw blade. Then they made the motor to move the blade.

Blaze showed off his new saw.
"I'm a Reciprocating Saw Monster Machine!"
he declared.

"Go get 'em, Blaze!" Darington cheered.
"Carve up those Robo Pumpkins!" shouted Stripes.

Blaze and AJ zoomed forward, and every time they spotted a Robo Pumpkin flying toward them, Blaze hit a ramp and flew into the air. Then he cut the pumpkin in half with his new saw.

BUZZZZ!

In no time at all, Blaze had cut up all the pumpkins. "We came, we *sawed*, we conquered!" shouted Blaze.

"Way to go, y'all!" said Starla. "Yay for Blaze!" shouted Zeg. "Thanks, guys," said Blaze. "Now come on! Our candy's just up ahead."

From the top of a hill, the Monster Machines spotted their candy buckets next to the barn.

"Woo-hoo!" Darington whooped. "We found our candy!"

But just then, they saw Crusher drive up to the buckets, laughing.

"Oh, no!" Starla cried. "We can't let Crusher get all our treats. We gotta do something!"

"Hey, I have an idea," Blaze said. "We can scare Crusher away with a super-spooky shadow!"

"Let's do it!" said AJ. He raised his cape and stepped in front of Blaze's bright lights.

"Nothing can stop me from getting their candy now!" Crusher hooted. "Not Blaze, not his friends, not even . . . that giant spooky bat! YAAHHH!"

Crusher zoomed away as fast as his tires could carry him.

"Hang on, Crusher! Wait for me!" yelled Pickle.

The Monster Machines cheered. "Yay! We did it!"

Blaze and his friends raced down to their candy buckets. Zeg started gobbling up his treats right away, and so did Stripes, Starla, and Darington. The candy was delicious!

"Happy Halloween, Blaze!" said AJ as he grabbed his bucket.

"You too!" said Blaze, tossing candy into his mouth.

Back in Axle City, Crusher spotted a box with an orange bow on the side of the road.

"Oooh!" he squealed. "I just know there's candy in there."

But when he opened it, the box was full of . . . tickling spiders! Giggling, they jumped on Crusher and started tickling him.

"Oh, no. . . . Ho, ho, ho! Ha, ha! Hee, hee, hee!" Crusher laughed uncontrollably. The trick was on him!